ADVANCED CHESS

David Norwood

Edited by Lisa Watts and Carol Varley
Designed by Richard Johnson

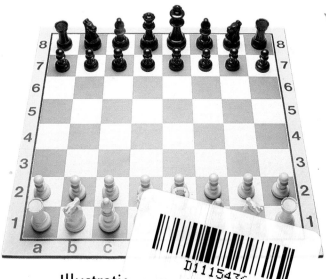

Illustratio... by Ian W...
Photographs by Jane Munro ...ly
With thanks to Sheila Jackson

D1115436

Contents

Cover photography by John Bellenis
Cover chess set supplied by Gareth Williams

First published in 1990 by Usborne Publishing. Ltd., Usborne House, 83-85 Saffron Hill, London, EC1N 8RT, England. © 1990, Usborne Publishing Ltd. The name Usborne and the devices ♀⊕ are Trade Marks of Usborne Publishing Ltd.

Printed in Portugal

Using this book

This book is an introduction to advanced chess techniques. It describes the aims of each stage of the game and alerts you to some of the common pitfalls. All the techniques are clearly explained with example games and moves. It is a good idea to follow the diagrams on a chess board if possible. This will help you to understand the principles explained in the book and use them in your own games.

Following the diagrams

The examples are fully illustrated throughout the book, using photographs and move-by-move diagrams. The chess pieces appear as symbols in the diagrams. These are shown on the right. When pieces move, they are shown on the squares they are about to leave. Red or green arrows, like those below right, point to their destination.

All moves are numbered in the diagrams, as on the board below. Chess moves are written in algebraic notation (explained on page 5), and they are highlighted in the text with bold print.

Diagram symbols

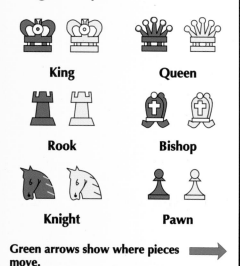

King   Queen

Rook   Bishop

Knight   Pawn

Green arrows show where pieces move.

A capture is shown as a red arrow, with a circle around the captured piece.

A hollow red arrow indicates an attack.

A hollow green arrow shows a potential move.

Chess terms

If you discover a chess term that you are unsure of, you can find a clear explanation in the glossary at the back of the book.

In the text, words that you may not understand are printed in italics to remind you that they are explained in the glossary.

Tips and tests

There are lists of useful chess tips at the end of most sections of the book to help you remember the essential points which have been covered. There are regular revision puzzles too, so that you can put your new skills to the test. Answers to these puzzles are at the back of the book.

Improving your game

A game of chess can usually be divided into three stages – the *opening*, the *middlegame* and the *endgame*. To improve your game you need to understand the aims and strategies of each stage.

The main features of the opening, the middlegame and endgame are described below, and you can discover more about all three later in the book. In this book, chess moves are written in *algebraic notation*. This is explained on the opposite page.

The opening

In the opening, the players develop their pieces to strong positions in preparation for the middlegame. Rooks and Bishops need to be brought from their starting positions so that they can attack. Pawns are positioned so that they control the centre of the board and the King must be kept safe near the edge of the board.

The middlegame

During the middlegame, players try to weaken each other by attacking their opponent's Pawns and capturing enemy pieces. It is important to make sure that any *exchanges* are to your advantage in the long term, so planning is vital. Your own King must be guarded and you should look for chances to attack the enemy King. The game may end at this stage if a King is exposed.

The endgame

In the endgame, players may have only a few pieces left so these need to be used very carefully. With fewer pieces to attack it, the King is less vulnerable and can join in the action. Pawns become more important and *promoting a Pawn* can become a major aim. Depending on which pieces are left on the board, and how well they are used, the game can end in a win or a draw.

Algebraic notation

Algebraic notation records moves using letters, numbers and symbols. The *ranks* on the board are numbered and the *files* are lettered. Each piece is referred to by its initial, except for the Knight which is N and Pawns for which no initial is used.

A move is written using the initial of the piece and the grid reference of the square it moves to. For example, **Nh3** means the Knight moves to square h3, and **Be3** means the Bishop moves to e3. For a Pawn, only the grid reference of its new position is given. For example, **f4** means a Pawn moves to f4.

Sometimes it is not clear which piece moves so in this case both the initial and file letter of the piece are given. For example, the move **Ne6** could be made by either of the Knights on this board. **Nce6** indicates that the move is made by the Knight on the c-file.

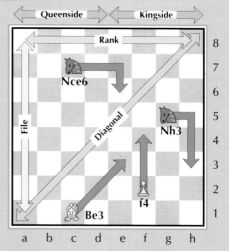

The moves are numbered and White's move is always written first. If Black's move is written without White's, dots are printed after the move number, for example, **4...Ng6**.

Symbols used in notation

Symbol	Example	
x	Bxh8	Bishop captures the piece on h8.*
+	Re7+	Rook moves to e7 and puts the King in check.
++	Re7++	Rook moves to e7 and checkmates the King.
0-0		Castles Kingside (files e-h).
0-0-0		Castles Queenside (files a-d).
!	Re3!	Rook makes a good move to e3.
?	Nf6?	Knight makes a bad move to f6.
=		The position is equal – neither side has the advantage.
(Q)	a8(Q)	White Pawn reaches the eighth rank and is promoted to a Queen.
(N)	d1(N)	Black Pawn promotes to a Knight.

Bxh8

0-0 Castles Kingside

0-0-0 Castles Queenside

* When a Pawn captures, only its file letter is given. For example, **bxc5** means that the Pawn on the b-file captures the piece on square c5.

Piece control

One of the best ways to improve your play is by developing a really good understanding of how each piece operates, its strengths and weaknesses, and what it can contribute at each stage of the game.

The next few pages give lots of useful information about how best to use your pieces.

The Bishop

Each player starts with a white-squared Bishop and a black-squared Bishop. Because they move only diagonally, they stay on these colours throughout the game. They can be powerful attacking pieces when they are not blocked in, so it is a good idea to bring them out early. This board shows how a Bishop can control the longest diagonal in two moves: **1. g3; 2. Bg2**, known as *fianchetto*. Notice how the Bishop is aimed like a cannon, protected on three sides by Pawns.

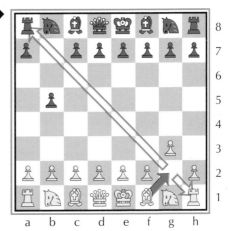

Strong Bishops

It is an advantage to keep both your Bishops (sometimes called the Bishop pair) until you are well into the game. Two Bishops working together control so many squares that they can dominate the board.

It is also important to avoid trapping your Bishops behind Pawns that have become *fixed* in their positions. It is therefore a good idea to bear your Bishops in mind when planning Pawn moves.

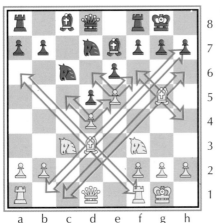

◄ Here, White's Bishops and Pawns are working as a team to control a large area of the board. The central Pawns are already fixed but White's Pawns are on black squares so they do not hinder the mobility of the white-squared Bishop. The white-squared Bishop controls the f1-a6 and b1-h7 diagonals, while the black-squared Pawns control squares c5, d6 and f6. A Bishop that works with its Pawns like this is called a *good-squared Bishop*. A Bishop that is trapped by its own Pawns and so has little mobility is called a *bad-squared Bishop*.

The Knight

Knights are the only pieces that can jump over other pieces, so you can bring them out early in the game. They are most powerful near the centre of the board, from where they can move to any of eight squares. A Knight at the side of the board can move to only four squares.

Because they can jump, Knights work well in blocked positions as they can manoeuvre to critical squares and stage surprise attacks. They are at their weakest in the endgame when their slow movement is a hindrance.

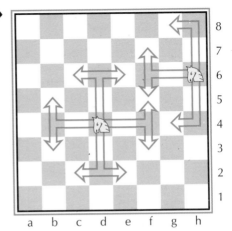

The Rook

Rooks work best on *open files* so, in the opening, you should move them to the centre, where usually you will have created open files with Pawn moves. Castling is one way to do this. Here, White's Rook controls the centre and puts the Black King in check in two moves: **1. 0-0; 2. Re1+**.

Two Rooks on the same rank or file – known as *double Rooks* – are strong as they support each other. They are especially strong on open files where they are not blocked in by Pawns (below left). They have extra power on the seventh rank as they can take pieces left on that rank (below right), or trap the enemy King on the back rank.

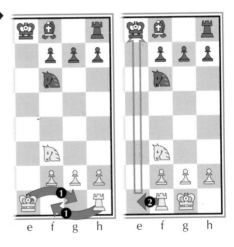

The Queen

The Queen is the most powerful piece on the board as it can move as many squares as you want in a straight line or diagonally. It is a dangerous and effective attacking piece, particularly if enemy pieces are badly co-ordinated or the King is exposed, as on this board. Here, the Queen moves to h4, attacking both the Black King and Rook.

It is best not to develop the Queen too early in the game, though, as it may well be attacked and forced to retreat. Because the Queen is so strong it must always avoid capture.

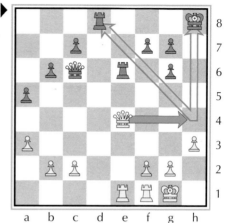

The King

Since the aim of chess is to capture the enemy King, you must keep your King safe at all times. During the opening it is best to move the King to the side by castling. If the King is left in the centre it becomes exposed to attack as the rest of the pieces are developed.

Here, the White King is well defended, protected by a wall of Pawns and a Knight on f3. Black's King is exposed, prevented from castling by the attacking Bishop on a3. (Remember, when castling, your King must not pass over any square that is attacked by your opponent.)

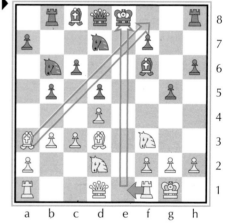

The King is strongest in the endgame when there are only a few pieces left and it can help checkmate the opponent or win pieces. On this board, the Black King is in a good position to win Pawns.

The King can move only one square at a time, so it has no attacking power during the early part of the game. If it is threatened you must immediately make a move to save it.

Piece values and exchanges

Each piece, except for the King, is given a value according to how powerful it is. The King has no value because when it is captured the game is over. It is useful to bear these values in mind when deciding whether it is worth losing a piece in order to capture an enemy piece.

Values

9 points

5 points

3 points

3 points

1 point

Exchanges

for

If you lose a piece of the same value as the piece you capture, it is a *fair exchange*.

for

If you lose a piece of less value than the piece you capture, you have the *exchange advantage*.

for

If you lose a piece of more value than the piece you capture, you have made a *sacrifice*.

These examples are from Black's point of view.

The piece values are a useful guide but you also have to bear in mind other factors. For example, in the exchange below (**1. Bxe7, Qxe7**), White captures Black's *good-squared Bishop* and loses the weaker of the two White Bishops. Although each side loses a Bishop, Black's Bishop was more mobile and therefore had more value. So in this case, White has the exchange advantage.

Similarly, a Pawn on the seventh rank, which is about to be *promoted*, is worth more than one point.

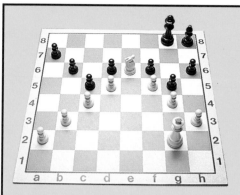

1. Black has a King and Bishop and White has a King and Knight. Which side is stronger?*

2. Black can move a Knight in order to gain strength. Which Knight should be moved and where to?*

3. Black to play. What would be the best move for the Black Queen?*

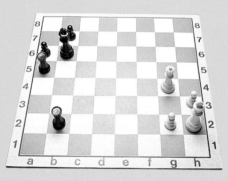

4. White to play. How can White win a Rook by moving the Queen?*

5. White can use the Bishop to capture the Black Knight. How?*

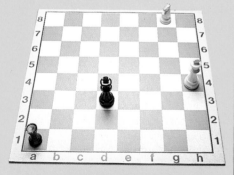

6. How can Black win the Knight and so leave White unable to win?*

Pawns

At the start of the game a Pawn is a minor piece but it can become the strongest piece if it reaches the other end of the board and is *promoted*.* So it is important to move your Pawns with care.

This page shows how the Pawn's role changes during the game. Over the page there are examples of strong *Pawn structures* to aim for and some weak positions to be avoided.

The Pawn's role

During the opening, the Pawns usually defend the centre of the board and play a fairly static role.

In this example, the White Pawns have claimed the centre and form a strong barricade. Notice how squares c5, d5, e5 and f5 are all inaccessible to Black's pieces.

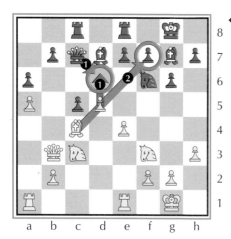

◀ In the middlegame, when development is complete, the Pawns become more active. Their role now is to drive off attacks from enemy pieces and move forward or sacrifice themselves to open attack lines for the Queen, Rooks and Bishops.

Here, White can sacrifice a Pawn and deliver check in two moves: **1.d6!**, **Qxd6**; **2. Bxf7+**. White gives up the Pawn to open the diagonal for the Bishop. White then moves the Bishop up the diagonal to put the Black King in check.

In the endgame, when few pieces are left on the board, Pawns can help the King to win material or to checkmate.

Here, Black has the material advantage; that is, Black's pieces add up to more points than White's in terms of piece value. However, White can gain strength by using the Pawns cleverly: **1. g6! fxg6**; **2. f6**. White sacrifices the g-Pawn, and the f-Pawn then advances. Black can now do

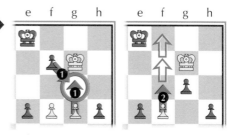

nothing to stop White's Pawn from reaching the eighth rank and promoting.

---

* *Although a Pawn is usually made into a Queen when it reaches the eighth rank, it can be promoted to any piece you choose.*

Strong Pawn positions

Pawns that are in a group can support each other. Here, Black's Pawns are in fewer groups, or *Pawn islands*, so they are stronger than White's.

In this example, White's Queenside Pawns are connected in a *Pawn chain*. To attack this chain, Black would have to attack the base Pawn on a2.

Passed Pawns are very strong as they can reach the other end of the board without meeting enemy Pawns on their own or adjacent files.

   Here, the Black King is too far away to stop White's a5 Pawn from reaching a8 and promoting. Beware though – enemy territory can be dangerous so your Pawns should usually be supported by other pieces.

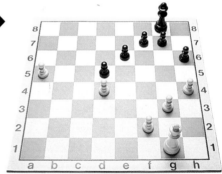

On this board, White's d-Pawn and e-Pawn have formed a central stronghold. By supporting each other they control more squares than they could if they worked independently.

A Pawn on the seventh rank is very strong. Here, the advancing White Pawns have pushed the Black King to the back rank. White has just moved to f7, delivering checkmate.

White's b3 Pawn is a *backward Pawn*. It has trailed behind and been left unsupported. If it advances, it will be captured by Black's c5 Pawn.

Here, White has three *isolated Pawns* – they cannot be defended by other Pawns. By playing **1...Rg4**, Black would be sure to win one of these.

◀ On this board, White's *double Pawns* on the b-file are weak. The back Pawn cannot advance until the front Pawn moves and the two Pawns cannot protect each other.

Black's *triple Pawns* are even worse. This time two Pawns must wait for the first Pawn to advance before they can move forward. Avoid trapping Pawns in this way.

Here, White's centre Pawns are *fixed*. The White e-Pawn is blocked by Black's e-Pawn and the Black Knight is preventing the White d-Pawn from moving up the board.

White's *hanging Pawns* on c4 and d4 are relying on *major pieces* rather than Pawns for protection. They have advanced without adequate support and are an easy target for Black.

13

The opening

During the first few moves of the game you should try to develop your pieces to good positions from which they can attack your opponent in the middlegame. The board below shows some of the better positions for the various pieces, and those to be avoided. The key opposite explains more about the positions shown.

On the next few pages, some famous opening strategies are described. These are series of moves which have been played and analysed for many years. They are named after chess players, or the tournaments at which they became famous.

On this board Black has made many mistakes. The Black pieces have no control of the centre and are placed at the sides of the board where they have limited power. Also, Black has taken no care to protect the King. In contrast, White has good piece development and a strong position.

It is important to bring your Rooks, Knights and Bishops into action as quickly as possible. Make sure that you do not begin to attack until you have done this. As a general rule, you should not move any piece more than once until you have finished your development.

Key to board

This key explains the good and bad positions on the board opposite. You can use this as a checklist or guide when you play your openings. If you follow these principles during the early moves of your game, you will handle the opening well and be fully prepared for the middlegame.

1 Develop Knights and Bishops towards the centre.

2 Castle early to keep the King safe.

3 Avoid hemmed-in Bishops and Rooks.

4 Aim to control the centre: put Pawns on d4 and e4 or d5 and e5. If you cannot do this, try to prevent your opponent from dominating the centre.

5 Place Rooks on *open files*, or those least blocked by Pawns.

6 Keep Knights away from the edge of the board.

7 Position your Queen for attack – but not too early as it may be attacked.

8 Do not leave your King exposed to attack – avoid moving the Pawns in front of your King too early as this may leave the King vulnerable.

9 Do not waste time on weak Pawn moves.

Famous openings

Famous openings can be divided into those for White, which try to retain the opening *initiative*, and those for Black, which aim to steal the initiative from White.

Because you can only guess your opponent's responses, famous openings are very flexible. Usually just one or two key moves give an opening its identity.

Some famous openings involve unusual development and moves that contradict the basic opening principles. Because of this, it is unwise to try to play out famous openings in your own game until you are completely sure of all the basic opening rules. Instead, study the mechanics of the openings to see how certain moves put pressure on the opponent and how particular attacks trigger certain replies.

By studying famous openings you can also see how the plans and action of the middlegame are shaped by decisions taken early in the game.

DID YOU KNOW? ● After each side has played three moves, the pieces could form any one of over nine million possible positions on the board. If these were photographed at a rate of one a minute, it would take over 17 years, day and night, to record all the positions.

● The total number of possible games lasting 40 moves each is greater than the number of atoms in the universe.

● The longest game theoretically possible is 5,949 moves.

The Spanish Opening

This popular opening is characterized by White's third move (3. Bb5). Black aims to neutralize White's opening *initiative* before adopting aggressive plans.

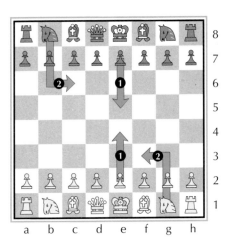

1. e4, e5; 2. Nf3, Nc6. Each side advances a Pawn towards the centre. The White Knight then attacks the Black e-Pawn and Black defends it.

3. Bb5, a6. The White Bishop attacks the Black Knight that is defending Black's e-Pawn. Black then attacks the Bishop with a Pawn.

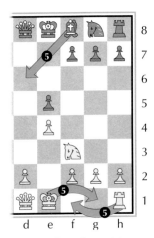

4. Bxc6, dxc6. White captures the Knight and Black takes the Bishop (a *fair exchange*). Black's Queen now has a *semi-open file* along which to attack but the Pawns are *doubled* – a weak position.

5. 0-0, Bd6. The White King castles and Black develops a Bishop to defend the e-Pawn.

6. d4, exd4; 7. Qxd4, f6. White brings out a Pawn to control the centre and Black captures it. The White Queen then captures the Black Pawn and Black moves a Pawn to f6 in order to block the Queen, which is now attacking g7.

8. b3! Be6. White moves the b-Pawn in preparation for *fianchetto*, and Black tries to complete development.

How each side stands

At the end of this opening, Black is still responding to White's moves, so White has retained the initiative. White has a slight positional advantage as the White pieces are slightly better placed than the Black. The White King has castled to safety and White has a Pawn in the centre of the board, as well as a *good-squared Bishop*, which occupies the opposite colour square to most of the Pawns. Also, the White Queen is dominating the centre of the board, backed up by the Rook on f1, which is ready to move to the *open* d-file.

Black, on the other hand, has not yet castled, has weak doubled Pawns on the c-file and a hemmed-in Queen.

However, Black still has both Bishops and the Pawn majority on the Queenside, which could be an advantage.

The King's Gambit

This is an opening for White. Although it begins in the same way as the Spanish Opening, White's second move – the gambit of the King's Bishop's Pawn (the f-Pawn) – gives this opening a character of its own.

A *gambit* is a strategy in which a piece is offered for sacrifice in order to gain advantage later in the game. In this opening, White sacrifices the f-Pawn to open up the f-file. White's moves are aggressive and it is difficult for Black to defend against them.

1. e4, e5; 2. f4, exf4. Both players advance a Pawn. White then offers the f-Pawn for sacrifice and Black captures it, accepting the gambit.

3. Nf3, Be7. White brings out a Knight to prevent the Black Queen from giving check from h4. Black then develops a Bishop.

4. Be2! Bh4+. White prepares to castle, but Black prevents this by advancing the Bishop to h4 and putting the White King in check.

5. Kf1, Be7. White moves the King out of check and Black moves the Bishop from h4, where it was a target for the White Knight.

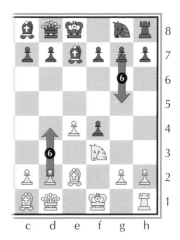

6. d4, g5. White claims the centre and attacks the f4 Pawn with a Bishop. Black defends f4 by advancing the g-Pawn to form a *Pawn chain*.

7. h4, g4. White attacks the base of the Pawn chain and Black advances the g-Pawn to attack White's Knight.

8. Ne5, h5. White brings out a Knight to attack Black's weak Pawns on f7 and g4. Black defends the g-Pawn.

9. Bc4, Rh7. White moves a Bishop to c4, from where it attacks the Pawn on f7. Black advances a Rook to defend f7.

How each side stands

After playing **10. Bxf4**, White controls the centre and has good piece development, as shown here. White also has space in which to manoeuvre and chances to attack the Black King.

Black has no central control and has barely begun piece development. However, Black can now play **10…d6**, attacking the Knight and opening the diagonal for the c8 Bishop.

A trick for Black

It is interesting to consider how Black could have changed the outcome of this opening with an early move. If possible, follow these moves on a chess board.

1. e4, e5; **2. f4, Bc5.** Black offers the e-Pawn as a *counter gambit*. If White accepts with **3.fxe5**, White will lose by the following sequence: **3…Qh4+**; **4.Ke2, Qxe4++.**

The Caro-Kann

This is an opening for Black that can be used in response to 1. e4. It is named after two famous 19th century players, H. Caro and M. Kann.

In this opening, Black challenges the centre in an unusual way and pays less attention to piece development. Black's plan is to establish a strong defence with a solid Pawn structure before beginning to attack. Black's first two moves give this opening its identity.

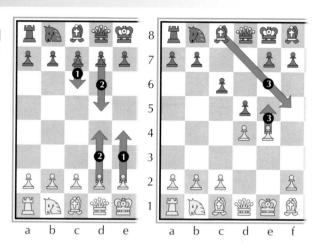

1. e4, c6; 2. d4, d5. Black allows White to take the centre and then issues a direct challenge to White's e-Pawn.

3. e5, Bf5. White does not *exchange* central Pawns but pushes the e-Pawn forward. Black develops the weaker of the two Bishops.

4. Bd3, Bxd3; 5. Qxd3, e6. In these two moves White's strongest Bishop is exchanged for Black's weaker Bishop. White should have avoided this exchange as it has given Black control of the white squares. Instead, White could have moved the Bishop to e2, or advanced the Kingside Pawns to g4, h4 and so on.

6. Nc3, Qb6. White develops a Knight, but Black, who has adopted an unusual plan, neglects normal development and brings out the Queen.

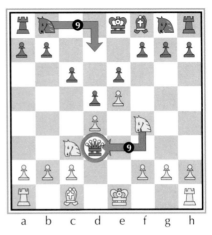

7. Nge2, Qa6; 8. Nf4, Qxd3. White continues with development and Black prepares to exchange Queens. White allows the exchange of Queens but this is an error since Black has the *positional advantage*, with a more mobile Bishop and strong Pawns.

9. Nxd3, Nd7=. Black *equalizes*. White no longer has the opening *initiative* and the *material* is level – both sides have the same pieces. Also, the strengths and weaknesses of each side are evenly matched, as explained below.

How each side stands

At this stage, with an even balance between the two sides, both players need to exploit their strengths in order to gain the advantage. In the long term, Black has more chance to control the centre by moving Pawns to c5 and f6. These Pawn moves must be carefully prepared and used when they will have most impact.

White, on the other hand, has slightly better development, although this is less significant after the exchange of

Queens. With no Queens on the board the Kings no longer need such tight

protection as their most threatening attackers are gone.

The King's Indian Defence

The key feature of this opening for Black is the immediate *fianchetto* of Black's King's Bishop. In the early moves, Black purposely allows White's Pawns to control the centre. Black then plots to undermine them, using the fianchettoed Bishop as a weapon.

1. d4, Nf6. White advances a central Pawn and Black develops a Knight, preventing White from taking the centre immediately with a Pawn move to e4.

2. c4, g6. White continues to aim for the centre by advancing the c-Pawn and Black pushes forward the g-Pawn in preparation for fianchetto.

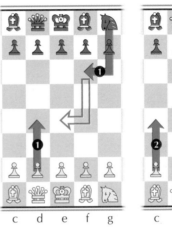

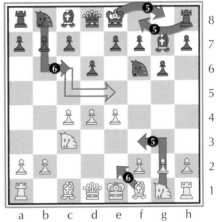

3. Nc3, Bg7; 4. e4, d6. After first moving the Knight as defence, White moves the e-Pawn. Black completes fianchetto, and advances the d-Pawn. Black's Pawn move is important as it frees the c8 Bishop, prevents White from moving a Pawn to e5 and prepares for a central challenge.

5. Nf3, 0-0; 6. Be2, Nc6. White develops a Knight and Black castles. White then continues with normal development and Black advances the Knight. Black is getting ready to challenge White's control of the centre by bringing a Pawn to e5; the Knight will give support.

a b c d e f g h

7. 0-0, e5. White castles and Black brings forward the e-Pawn as planned, threatening White's *Pawn centre*. White could have avoided this challenge by pushing the d-Pawn forward to d5. However, this move would have been risky: if Black's f6 Knight moved, the a1-h8 diagonal would be left open for the fianchettoed Bishop.

8. d5, Ne7. White advances the d-Pawn to block the centre as the dangerous fianchettoed Bishop is now obstructed on both e5 and f6. The Black Knight then retreats.

9. h3, Ne8! White advances the h-Pawn to prevent Black from playing **9...Ng4.** This move would clear the way for a Pawn advance to f5. Instead the Black Knight backs off to e8.

How each side stands

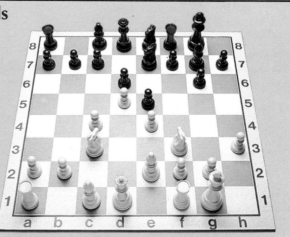

At this point Black's plan is working well. Next, Black will play **10...f5**. If White captures the f-Pawn with **11. exf5**, Black can reply with **11...gxf5**. Black will then control the central squares and the powerful fianchettoed Bishop will be free again. Black is also ready to advance Pawns down the Kingside.

All is not lost for White, though. White has more manoeuvring space than Black and can still gain the overall advantage by defending well on the Kingside and advancing the Queenside Pawns.

The middlegame

When both sides have protected the King and developed their pieces to positions from which they can attack or defend, the middlegame begins. Both players become more aggressive as they try to weaken one another's position and gain the advantage.

In the middlegame it is important to assess your own position on the board, identify your opponent's weakest points and form a strategy to exploit them.* The example strategies on the next few pages show some ways in which you might do this.

Middlegame example 1

On this middlegame board, White has the better development. White's Rooks dominate the central files and White also has more space in which to manoeuvre. At this point, each side has lost a Bishop and a Pawn.

It is White's turn. White plans to open up the b1-h7 diagonal so that the White Queen can attack the Black King, or the Knight on d7.

1. e5, Nh5. White moves the e-Pawn ▶ to open up the diagonal and forces Black to move the Knight on f6 out of the line of attack. This Knight was crucial to Black's defence as it protected the Knight on d7 and the Pawn on h7.

A piece which is relied on too heavily for defence, like the Knight in this example, is said to be *overloaded*.

2. Qd3, g6; **3. Qxd7**. First, White ▶ moves the Queen to d3, threatening checkmate with **3. Qxh7** and attacking the unprotected Knight on d7. Black advances the g-Pawn, creating an escape square for the vulnerable King. White then captures the Knight, leaving Black with a *material disadvantage* and grave prospects. Through careful planning, White is now in a strong position.

You can learn more about planning on pages 35-39.

Middlegame example 2

On this board White has the *material advantage* but Black's pieces are very well placed. Black plans to achieve a winning position by opening up the h-file. It is Black's turn to move.

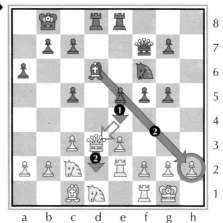

1...e4; 2. Qd2, Bxh2+. Black's first Pawn move opens the diagonal for the Bishop and threatens the White Queen. White then moves the Queen out of danger and Black captures the Pawn on h2 – putting the White King in check and opening the h-file for Black's Rooks, Queen and Knight.

3. Kxh2, Qh5+. The White King captures its attacker but is put in check again by Black's Queen, which moves to the open h-file.

4. Kg1, Ng4. The White King retreats. Black could have captured White's Queen with **4...Rxd2** but instead prepares for an attack on a greater prize – the White King.

5. Qxd8, Rxd8. Faced with imminent checkmate (**5...Qh2++**). White can only stall for time. By taking the Black Rook, however, White merely loses the Queen.

6. Rfe1, Qh2+. White moves a Rook to create a temporary retreat for the King and so avoid immediate checkmate. The Black Queen moves to give check from h2.

7.Kf1, Qh1++. The doomed White King backs away but is immediately checkmated by the Black Queen.

Middlegame example 3

Here, White has some power over the centre, with the Rook controlling the open e-file. The Black King has castled and is safe but the Black Knight is badly positioned. White's best plan is to break up the Black Kingside Pawns and penetrate Black's defences with the Queen and Rook.

1. Bxf6, gxf6. White's Bishop takes the Black Knight and Black captures White's Bishop with a Pawn. This is a *fair exchange* but White has drawn a Pawn from the Black King's defences.

2. Re3!, Rfe8. White moves a Rook to e3 – a good move as, from this square, the Rook can cross to the h-file, or dominate the e-file. Black, forced to act defensively, moves a Rook to challenge the e-file.

White's next two moves are **3. Rh3** and **4. Qh5** – bringing two powerful pieces to back each other up along the h-file. Regardless of Black's response, White will, at least, win the h-Pawn and seriously weaken Black's defences.

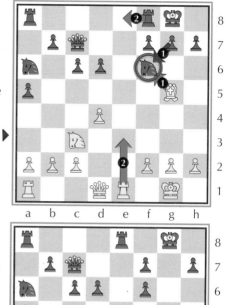

Middlegame example 4

In this example, Black's plan is to play for central control by capturing White's *good-squared Bishop*. It is Black's turn to move.

1...Nxd3. Black takes the Bishop with a Knight. **2. Qxd3, Nd5**. Black then loses the Knight to the Queen (a fair exchange). Black's f6 Knight leaps to d5, from where it can control the centre as White has no c-Pawn or e-Pawn to chase it.

In two moves Black has weakened White's position and gained power.

26

Middlegame example 5

In this example, White's plan is to open the h-file and focus the attack on the Kingside.

1. h4, Qa5. White advances a Pawn up the h-file and Black mobilizes the Queen. Black cannot block the White Pawn with **1...h5** because the Black Pawn would be taken with **2. gxh5**, opening up the h-file. Black is also prevented from moving the Knight on f6 as this Knight is shielding the Black Queen from the g5 Bishop. By moving the Queen, Black releases the f6 Knight and provokes action on the Queenside.

White can continue the attack down the h-file with **2. h5**, and **3. Bh6** (to remove Black's defending Bishop on g7), then **4. hxg6**, forcing Black to play

4...hxg6. This exchange of Pawns will open up the h-file and leave Black in a dangerous position.

Test yourself

1. Here, Black has the positional advantage, with more mobile Pawns in fewer *islands*. The Pawns are also well placed on opposite-coloured squares to the Bishop. Black's next move can threaten the White Queen and lead to material gain. What should Black's move be?*

2. On this board, White is stronger, with more Pawns in fewer islands. White will probably win the game – one way would be by doubling Rooks on the b-file. First, though, White can capture a Black Bishop. Which one should be captured?*

*Puzzle answers on pages 61-63.

The endgame

As more pieces are *exchanged*, the game approaches the endgame. In this phase, opportunities for checkmate usually become fewer, especially if the players have exchanged Queens. Now the King can venture from its defended position to join in the attack, or help to *promote a Pawn* – one of the main aims in the endgame.

Mobilizing the King

Here, both sides need to bring their King into action. Black's outlook is bleak as the King cannot attack any of White's Pawns and the Bishop is powerless. In contrast, White has a *good-squared Bishop*, a strong Pawn structure and can mobilize the King. By advancing diagonally, the White King can attack square a5, allowing the Bishop to capture Black's most vulnerable Pawn. In the middlegame, the threat of checkmate would have made such a King advance impossible.

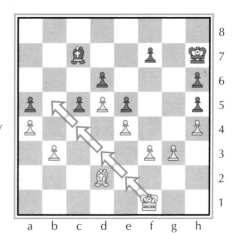

King and Pawn endgames

When each side has only the King and some Pawns, you need to calculate moves carefully in order to promote a Pawn before your opponent. Here, Black can promote as follows: **1.Kd4, Kg5**; **2.Kc5, Kxg4**; **3. Kxb5, Kxh5**;

4. Kxa4, Kg4. Black's Pawn can now march up the h-file and become a Queen. White is unable to promote the a-Pawn because, by the time it reaches a8, that square will be controlled by Black's new Queen.

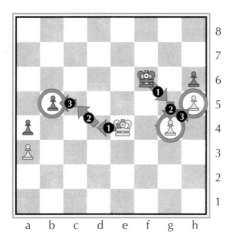

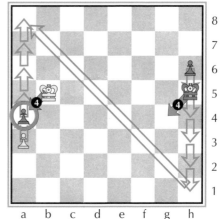

Gaining the opposition

When the two Kings are facing each other along a file, with only one square in between, the player who moved last is said to have the *opposition*. The other King must move back or to the side as an advance would be illegal. You can sometimes make a stalling move, called *losing a tempo*, in order to gain the opposition.

In a King and Pawn endgame you can use the opposition to steer the enemy King away from the *queening square* and so allow your Pawn to promote, as shown in this example.

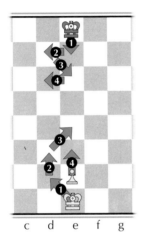  

8
7
6
5
4
3
2
1

c d e f g   c d e f g   c d e f g

1. Kd2, Ke7; **2. Kd3, Kd7**. (If Black played **2...Ke6**, White's next move would gain the opposition.) **3. Ke4, Ke6**. Now Black has the opposition, but White can regain it by losing a tempo: **4. e3!** Black must now sidestep with **4...Kd6**. The moves continue with **5. Kf5, Ke7**. (If Black played **5...Kd5** then White would play **6. e4+**.)

6. Ke5 (keeping the opposition), **6...Kd7**; **7. Kf6** (White must not push the Pawn to e4 yet, as **7...Ke7** would then gain the opposition for Black) **7...Kd6**; **8.e4**. Now the White King controls the squares ahead of the Pawn and it can progress in safety. The Black King can now do nothing to stop the Pawn from promoting.

An alternative ending

d e f   d e f

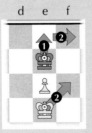 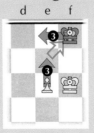

It is vital that the King advances in front of the Pawn. If White had played **1. e4**, the players may have reached the positions shown far left. Black could then draw, with: **1...Ke8!**; **2. Kf6, Kf8**; **3. e7+, Ke8**. Black's last move makes it impossible for the White Pawn to promote, so White must abandon it or play **4. Ke6**, leading to *stalemate*.

29

Rook endgames

In a Rook endgame, each side has only a Rook, a few Pawns and the King. This is the most common type of endgame.

With only one *major piece* left, apart from the King, you need to use it to the full, so you should try to place your Rook on an *open file* where it will have the greatest influence. Another key to winning Rook and Pawn endgames is to create a *passed Pawn*. Your Rook and Pawns need to work together very carefully to achieve this.

The examples on these two pages outline three techniques that will help you to win Rook and Pawn endgames.

Keeping active

On this board the Black and White Pawn and King positions are symmetrical. Only the places of the Rooks are different – but this is all-important. White's Rook is superbly placed: it is attacking Black's a5, f6 and h5 Pawns.

Black's Rook has no mobility. It has to defend the f6 and h5 Pawns and, if it moves, one of these Pawns will be lost. Also, the Black King must stay on b6 or a6 to defend the a5 Pawn. White's Rook dominates the board; it controls Black's moves and the White King has total freedom.

Creating passed Pawns

A passed Pawn has two uses. You can make a direct attempt to *promote* it or you can use it as a decoy: while your opponent is attempting to stop your passed Pawn from promoting, you can capture the Pawns whose defence has been abandoned.

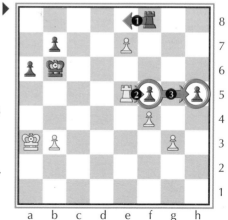

On the board on the right it is Black's turn to move. Black plays **1...Re8** to prevent White from promoting the Pawn on e7. White can now switch plans and capture the f5 and h5 Pawns. White loses the passed Pawn on e7, but now has two connected passed Pawns on f4 and g3.

Rooks and passed Pawns

Be careful to keep your Rook behind a passed Pawn or it will block the Pawn's advance, as shown in the example on the right. Here, Black appears to be winning as White's pieces cannot move.* However, the Black Rook is in front of the passed Pawn on a2. By remaining on a1, the Rook stops the Pawn from promoting, but if it moves, White can play **Rxa2**.

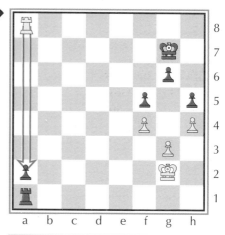

Black could only promote by moving the King to b2 or b3 to defend the Pawn so that the Rook can move. Black cannot achieve this though, as the King has no cover and would be constantly checked by White's Rook. So Black has no winning plan.

In contrast, on this board the Black Rook is behind the passed Pawn and it is White's Rook that is trapped on a1. Black needs to bring the King to b2 to force the Rook to move and allow the Pawn to promote. White can only prevent this by moving the King to the Queenside, but by doing so, White will abandon the defence of the Kingside Pawns, which can then be mopped up by Black's King. Here, Black is in an excellent position to win pieces.

Endgame tips

Many of the principles of Rook and Pawn endgames also apply to Knight, Bishop and even Queen endgames.

• Use your King. Note that in all the above examples the King plays a vital role in carrying out the plan.

• Remember that in most endgames, the King changes from a piece to be defended to an attacking piece.

• Keep pieces active; combine both attack and defence as best you can.

• Guard your passed Pawns – and try to prevent your opponent from getting a passed Pawn too.

• Be sure you can support passed Pawns without making your pieces passive, as in the first example opposite.

---

* Can you see what would happen if the King or Rook moved?
Puzzle answers on pages 61-63.

Winning, drawing or losing

Endgames have been studied by chess analysts for centuries and the outcome of endgames with certain combinations of pieces is well known. It is useful to bear the winning combinations in mind when *exchanging* pieces or going into the endgame. These two pages show some common winning, losing and drawing combinations. In each example, Black is attacking and White defending. There is a chart showing other combinations on page 34.

 against

A King with two Bishops is an easy win against a lone King. Keep your pieces together and corner the King, trapping it in a mating net (see Endgame techniques below). Here, Black plays **1...Be4+**. White must then play **2. Ka1**. Black's next move, **2...Bd4**, is checkmate.

The King, Bishop and Knight can win against the King but it is tricky. On the board below, Black checkmates with **1...Nc1; 2. Ka1, Bd4++**, forcing the King into a corner of the same colour as the Bishop's square. This is called the dangerous corner (see Endgame techniques below).

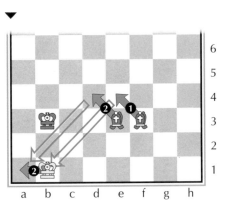

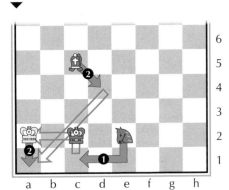

Endgame techniques

In both the examples on this page, you have to form a *mating net* to win. In a mating net your pieces are placed so that wherever the King moves, it is trapped. It is impossible to checkmate the King in the centre of the board when you have only a few pieces, so it is vital that you corner the King.

Note how, in the second example, the attacking Bishop is black-squared and the King is checkmated in a black corner. This is the dangerous corner. It is impossible to force checkmate in a non-dangerous corner – a corner of the opposite colour to that of your Bishop's square. If the enemy King is aiming for a non-dangerous corner, try to force it across to a dangerous corner so that you can form a mating net and win the game.

An interesting position is shown here.
Black has a Bishop and Pawn but,
surprisingly, this is not enough to win.
This is because the Rook's Pawn (the
one that starts on the same file as the
Rook) is heading for h1 – a white
square which the Bishop cannot
control. Black cannot force the White
King to move from this corner and the
Pawn will not be able to *promote*. This
situation is called the Bishop and
wrong Rook's Pawn, and is always a
draw if the enemy King can reach the
vital corner in time.

If the Bishop was on g6, Black would
be able to win easily as the Bishop

could control h1. In the example
shown here the game will end in
stalemate, for example with:
1. Kg1, Bd4+; 2. Kh1, h2 stalemate.

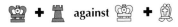
For this combination to result in a
draw, the side with the *minor piece*
needs to aim for the non-dangerous
corner – as White has done here. In
this position, Black cannot make
progress. White should move the
Bishop between a7 and b8. If Black
prevents this by moving a Rook to f8,
White can move the King to and fro
between a8 and a7. Black cannot
break this repetitive pattern without
forcing stalemate – with **1...Ba7**;
2. Rf8+, Bb8; 3. Kb6 for example.

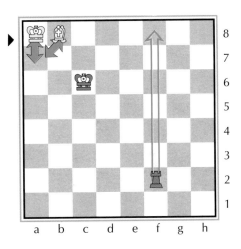

This combination can be a draw as
long as the side with the minor piece
(White in this example) keeps the King
and Knight together.

On this board, although the Knight
prevents immediate checkmate from
1...Rd1++, White is vulnerable as the
King and Knight are separated. Black
can move **1...Rd2** forcing the Knight to
c4 or a4 to avoid capture. Black can
then play **2...Rd1++**.

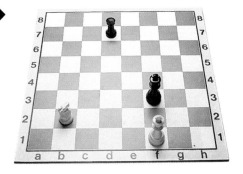

Other winning or drawing combinations

♚ + ♗/♞ against ♚	**Draw**	It is impossible to construct a mating net with a King and Bishop, or King and Knight.
♚ + **Rook's** ♙ against ♚ **Pawn**	**Draw**	This is always a draw as long as the defending King can advance in front of the enemy Pawn, preventing it from promoting.
♚ + ♞ + ♞ against ♚	**Draw**	The Knights cannot force the enemy King into a mating net.
♚ + ♜ against ♚	**Win**	The King and Rook can force the enemy King to one side and easily give checkmate.
♚ + ♛ against ♚ + ♜	**Win**	You can use the King and Queen to push the enemy King to the side, then try to *fork* the King and Rook with the Queen.

Test yourself

1. White to play. How can White promote a Pawn and win?*

2. How can White avoid losing this endgame? White to play.*

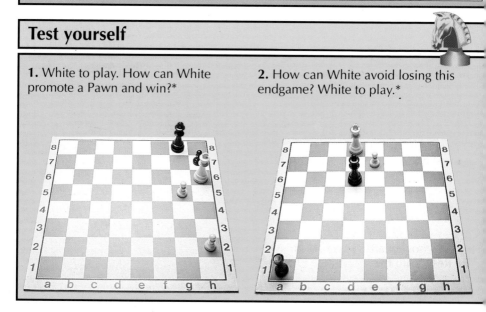

Planning

In order to improve your game you should try to make sure that every one of your moves is part of a plan. The examples on pages 24-27 illustrate the benefits of planning in the middlegame; the examples on the next few pages deal with the art of planning at other stages of the game.

The first stage of any plan is to decide on your aim. Checkmate is rarely a realistic short term goal, but you may be able to *promote a Pawn*, make an *exchange* or improve your defence. Having decided on your objective, the next stage is to find the best way to achieve it.

Planning example 1

The best way to decide on a plan is to search for weaknesses in your opponent's position. A weak *Pawn structure*, for example, is an excellent target for attack. If, on the other hand, your own Pawns are weak, a more useful objective may be to improve their defence.

Forming the plan

On this endgame board the *material* is level (both sides have the same pieces left) but White has a weak Pawn structure, with isolated Pawns on the Queenside. Black has to decide on a plan which will exploit the weakness in White's Pawn structure and White has to adopt a defensive plan. It is Black's turn to move.

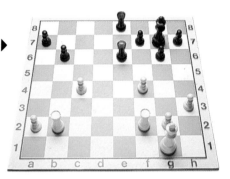

Carrying out the plan

First Black can attack the weak c4 Pawn with **1...Rc8**. White could defend with **2. Rbc2** but this would enable Black to capture the c-Pawn by doubling Rooks on the c-file (**2...Rec6**). So instead White chooses an alternative defensive move – **2. Rb4**. Now, if Black does double the Rooks on the c-file, White can defend by playing **3. Rc2**.

Black now changes plan and plays **2...Re4!** With this move Black will win either the c4 or f4 Pawn – thanks to careful planning.

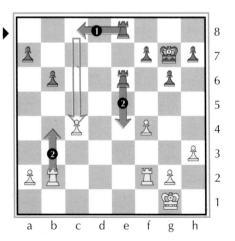

Planning example 2

In the planning example on the previous page, Black's plan involved only a couple of moves to exploit an obvious weakness in White's Pawn structure. Although most games require more sophisticated plans, the attack or defence of Pawn structure is still very often the central objective – as you can see from the model game that follows.

Forming the plan

This board shows the positions of the pieces after the fifth move of a version of the Modern Benoni opening.* Each side has lost a Pawn: White has lost the c-Pawn and taken Black's e-Pawn.

It is early in the game and neither side is in a position to give checkmate or win material. However, there are already several features around which each side can make plans. White has more central Pawns and so will want to build on this strength.

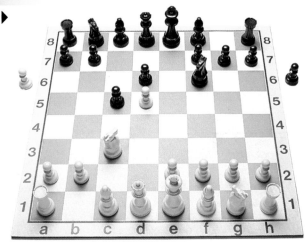

Black, on the other hand, is weak in the centre, having already lost the e-Pawn, but strong on the Queenside. In addition, Black's King's Bishop is blocked in, so Black will probably plan to mobilize this Bishop with a *fianchetto* move.

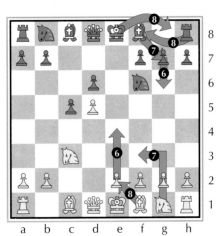

Carrying out the plan

◀ White's next move is **6. e4**, gaining strength in the centre of the board and opening the f1-a6 diagonal to give the Bishop mobility. Black's King's Bishop has little mobility on the a3-f8 diagonal, which is blocked by the Pawns on c5 and d6. Black therefore moves **6...g6** in preparation for fianchetto.

Both sides continue with sensible developing moves as shown on the board on the left:

7. Nf3, Bg7; 8. Be2, 0-0.

* *Most famous openings have several different versions. An alternative version of this opening appears on page 47.*

9. 0-0, Re8. White now castles to move the King from the centre file, and Black brings a Rook to the *semi-open* e-file, threatening the e4 Pawn. Like the fianchetto, this move is determined by the Pawn structure – in this case, the absence of Black's e-Pawn.

Both sides can now concentrate on their main plan: White aims to dominate the centre with Pawn advances to f4 and e5, and Black is planning to advance on the Queenside, and create a *passed Pawn*.

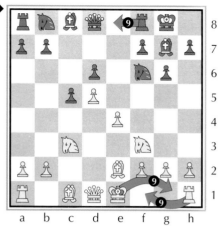

10. Nd2, a6. White moves the Knight to prepare for Pawn expansion in the centre. Black advances a Queenside Pawn as planned. Note how Black's fianchettoed Bishop on g7 is already positioned to support the Pawns as they near their *queening squares*.

Next, Black plans to move **11...b5**, to control squares a4, b4, c4 and d4 and so dominate the Queenside. However, White anticipates this and plays **11. a4!** (Although White wants to expand in the centre, it is more important to stop Black's advance to b5.) Instead, Black plays **11...Nbd7**, gaining control of e5.

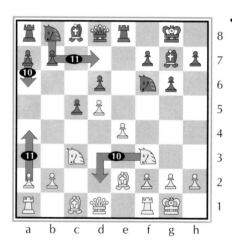

Taking stock

Look again at the starting positions to see how the Pawn structure affected each side's plans. White's plan was based on strong central Pawns, and Black's on a Queenside Pawn majority.

Pawn structure also dictated piece development – such as Black's Bishop and Rook advances. Note how Black's c8 Bishop was left undeveloped because White's Pawns left it no active square to move to.

Continuing the plan

Now study the positions on the board after Black's eleventh move. Consider the objective of each side: Black is still planning to advance the b-Pawn to b5 and White, after moving the f-Pawn, intends to push forward the e-Pawn.

Both sides need to support their planned advances as well as possible. What preparations could the players make to help them achieve their objectives?*

*Puzzle answers on pages 61-63.

Planning example 3

In the following example, neither side has any immediate targets – the Kings are well defended and the pieces are adequately protected. Again, studying the Pawn structure provides the basis for a plan.

White's Pawn structure is fairly solid but Black has an isolated Queen's Pawn on d5. This Pawn is a weakness. Although it creates space for Black's other pieces, it cannot be defended by Pawns.

Forming the plan

It is White's move. A reasonable long term plan for White is to capture the d-Pawn. Black, however, is trying to advance this Pawn in order to exchange it. It has no useful role, so should be exchanged for White's e-Pawn.

White must construct a plan to take the d-Pawn. *Isolated Pawns* are weaker if they cannot advance, so first White must try to block the d-Pawn. The square in front of an isolated Pawn is a safe outpost for the other side.

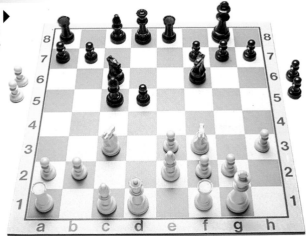

Black has no c-Pawn or e-Pawn and so cannot challenge square d4. White should therefore devise a plan to secure this square, while continuing to develop other pieces.

Carrying out the plan

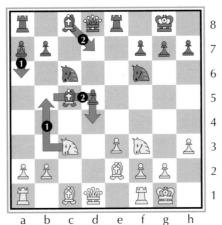

◀ **1. Nb5! a6.** White's Knight is aiming for d4. The f3 Knight could have moved there immediately but Black would then have played **1...Nxd4.** Then, after **2. exd4** both sides would have a similar Pawn structure and White's plan would be useless. With the next moves, **2. Nd4, Bd7,** White takes square d4 and Black brings out a Bishop. Black has no obvious plan: Black's first two moves were pointless as the White Knight was clearly heading for d4, and the Black Bishop has no function on the a4-e8 diagonal.

3. b3!, Rb8; **4. Bb2**. White's Queenside
fianchetto mobilizes the Bishop, which
was unable to move on the blocked
c1-h6 diagonal. On the long a1-h8
diagonal the Bishop can reinforce the
blockade on d4. Again, Black's move
was pointless – the Rook has no future
on a closed file, blocked by its own
Pawn. It really belongs on the *open*
c-file.

By studying the Pawn structure and
planning carefully, White has gained
the advantage in just a few moves.
Having blockaded the d5 Pawn, White
can now consider plans to attack it.

Test yourself

1. Consider the positions after
White's fourth move in the above
example. The next stage of White's
plan is to capture the d-Pawn, so
White has to prepare for this. What
are the best positions for the White
Rooks in order to help with this
plan?*

2. It is White's move. What plan
should White adopt and why?
Remember, identify Black's weakness,
then work out a plan to exploit it.*

Planning tips

• Look for easy targets such as an
exposed King, undefended pieces,
double Pawns or isolated Pawns, and
find ways to exploit them.

• Look at your own position and
rectify any glaring weaknesses.

• If there are no easy targets and your
position is fairly sound, look for
opportunities to create *passed Pawns*,
and consider possible sacrifices and
tactics.**

• If none of the above is feasible,
consider long term plans. Study the
Pawn structure to work out the best
positions for your pieces.

• Be alert to your opponent's moves
and try to guess the plan behind them.
Find ways to foil your opponent's plan
whilst pursuing your own.

• Do not be afraid to switch plans if
necessary. Keep flexible and do not
embark on a long and difficult plan if
you are not sure it will work.

* Puzzle answers on pages 61-63.
** See pages 42-45.

Defence

Throughout the game, all of your pieces should be working together to defend and support each other, but the most important piece to defend is, of course, the King.

In most cases, King defence is straightforward: you need to make sure that it never becomes exposed along files or diagonals and, if enemy pieces begin to crowd in on your King, you should fend them off. There are certain situations, though, when an apparently well-defended King can be the victim of a mating attack. Some of these are described here.

Back rank mate

◀ Here, Black has the *material advantage* and the Black King is barricaded by a wall of Pawns. However, White can force checkmate. Follow the moves to see how this is possible.

Notice how Black is forced into checkmate on the eighth rank (known as *back rank mate*). This occurs because the Pawns that are defending the Black King are also trapping it on the back rank. You can guard against back rank mate by moving the h-Pawn one square to give the King a retreat – as White has done here.

1. Qxd8

1...Rxd8; 2. Re8+

2...Rxe8

3. Rxe8++

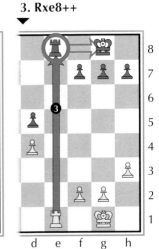

Exchanging the fianchettoed Bishop

If you *fianchetto* your Bishop so that it ▶
sits in front of your King, avoid
exchanging it, except for the Bishop
that occupies the same colour square.
If you trade it for the Bishop on the
opposite colour square, your opponent
has control of the critical diagonal in
front of your King.

Here, White has exchanged the
white-squared fianchettoed Bishop on
g2 for Black's black-squared Bishop.
The h1-a8 diagonal is now completely
controlled by Black's Queen and
white-squared Bishop. Black can now
give checkmate on g2 or h1.

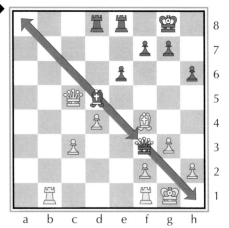

Defence tips

- See if you can divert an attack on
your own pieces by attacking your
opponent's King or other pieces.

- Do not give your opponent *open files*
or diagonals that lead to your King.

- Do not let your opponent bring a lot
of pieces close to your King.

- If under heavy attack, exchanging
Queens, as described below, may ease
the situation.

- Look after the fianchetto Bishop as
described above.

- To avoid a back rank mate, provide
your King with an escape square.

Exchanging Queens

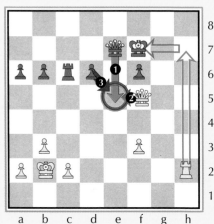

◀ Here Black is under heavy attack – the
Black King is exposed and threatened
with **1. Rh7+**. Without swift defensive
action Black will either be checkmated
or lose the Queen. In this situation,
Black's best means of defence is to play
1...Qe5+, forcing the exchange of
Queens – **2. Qxe5, dxe5**.

Now, if White plays **3. Rh7+**, the
Black King can simply advance, with
3...Ke6. The Black King is able to
support the advance of the e-Pawn and
f-Pawn and can also help capture
White's f-Pawn.

Tactical combinations

You need to be constantly on the lookout for ways to gain the advantage over your opponent. To succeed, you often need to use tactical combinations. These are series of moves that force your opponent to make certain replies. The aim may be *material* gain, *promoting a Pawn*, a better position or perhaps checkmate.

Tactical combinations often involve the use of *sacrifices* and devices such as *pins, forks, skewers* and *discovered attacks*. Be wary if a piece of yours is caught in one of these attacks and look very closely to see what your opponent is trying to do. It is possible that you are about to become the victim of a tactical combination which could lead to your downfall.

Combination 1

On the board on the right, it is White's ▶ turn to move. White has fewer pieces but can use a tactical trick to win material.

By playing **1. Bc7**, White reveals a *discovered check* by the White Rook. By moving to c7 White's Bishop does the maximum amount of damage to Black as, from this position, it attacks the Black Queen. Black is forced to move the King out of check first, so cannot avoid losing the Queen with White's next move.

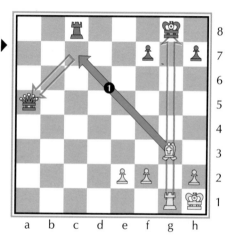

Combination 2

Although this combination is only two ◀ moves long, it features a pin, a sacrifice and a Knight fork.

White plays **1. d3** to free the c1 Bishop. However, this move also opens the diagonal on which both the White King and Queen are aligned – so this is a perfect place for Black to deal a tactical blow.

Black plays **1...Bb4!**, pinning the Queen. The Bishop is undefended, but Black has planned a combination which will sacrifice this Bishop in order to trap the Queen in a Knight fork, as described at the bottom of the opposite page.

42

Combination 3

Here, White uses a pin to force a series of moves and win material. Black played **1...Bg4** last move. Although this attacked White's Queen, it was a blunder. The only piece defending the Black Bishop is the Knight on f6 – and this piece is pinned to the Queen. If the Knight moves, the Queen is exposed to attack by the White Bishop. White can exploit this pin, as shown below.

White can play **2. Bxf6!** If Black then captures the Bishop on f6 with **2...Qxf6**, White can play **3. Qxg4**, winning a piece.

If, on the other hand, Black replies to **2. Bxf6!** by moving **2...Bxd1**, White can play **3. Bxd8** and the two sides exchange Queens.

Now, if Black's next move is **3...Bxc2**, capturing a Pawn, White can mirror the move with **4. Bxc7** and so remain one piece ahead.

---

2. Qxb4. White has to accept the sacrifice or Black will play **3...Bxc3+**. This forces White's Queen to square b4 – the ideal position for a Knight fork from c2. Black plays **2...Nxc2+**, bringing the Knight to c2, from where it forks the Queen and King. The King must move, so Black takes the Queen.

As this example shows, you should never leave both your King and Queen on an open diagonal that can be controlled by the enemy Bishop.

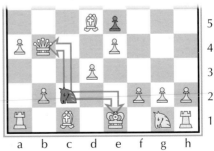

More tactical combinations

Tactical moves frequently centre around hot-spots on the board such as the King, or a Pawn that is close to *promoting* – as in the examples on these two pages.

Combination 4

On this board, White's last move was **Bc4**, pinning the Queen to the King. However, this tactical blow from White fails to a more subtle tactical combination from Black, which sacrifices the Queen to achieve *back rank mate*. Black plays **1...Qxc4!** offering up the Queen.

White has to take the Queen (**2. Rxc4**) to prevent Black from playing **2...Qxc1+**. Black can now continue with the next stage of the combination by playing **2...Rb1+**.

White's only way to get the King out of check is to play **3. Rc1**, to block the path of the Black Rook. Black can now remove the White Rook with **3...Rxc1++** and checkmate the King, as shown below.

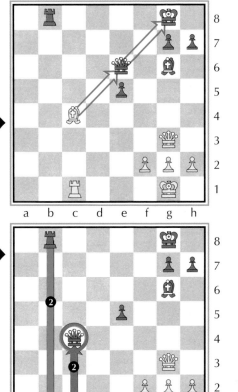

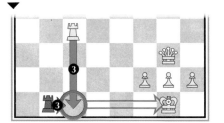

Notice how, in the final position, White's Pawns trap the White King instead of protecting it. Remember, to avoid this situation it is a good idea to play a move such as **h3** early in the game, giving your King an escape square.

Tactical tips

- Analyse tactical combinations carefully before you put them into practice – they may backfire as in Combination 4 above.

- Before using a tactical combination involving a *sacrifice*, make certain that you will not lose more *material* than you gain.

Combination 5

Here, White has just played **1. Rf2**, attacking the Black Bishop. Black cannot defend the Bishop and if it moves, the f5 Pawn will be lost. So Black plays **1...g3**, offering the Bishop as a sacrifice in order to promote a Pawn.

If White takes the Bishop with **2. Rxf4**, Black will play **2...g2**. The g-Pawn will be able to promote even though White is a Rook up because it guards f1 and the f5 Pawn controls square g4, as shown bottom right.

If White played **2. Rg2**, ignoring the Bishop, Black could play **2...Bd6+**. Black's Pawns are well advanced and supported by a Bishop so White cannot prevent promotion.

Test yourself

1. White to move. What tactic should White employ to achieve a winning position in two moves?*

2. White's move. White is seriously behind on material but can force checkmate in three moves. How?*

*Puzzle answers on pages 61-63.

Sacrifices

There are two types of sacrifice: the *calculative* and the *intuitive* sacrifice. In a calculative sacrifice a piece is given up for immediate benefit – to win a piece of greater value, perhaps, or to give checkmate. There are several examples of this type of sacrifice in the previous chapter, on tactical combinations.

Intuitive sacrifice is much more complex as the gain is not immediately apparent. The benefit of an intuitive sacrifice may be, for instance, a long term attack opportunity or an improvement in the position and mobility of your pieces.

Below is a simple calculative sacrifice and the next few pages analyse a game which features an intuitive sacrifice.

Calculative sacrifice

It is White's turn to move. Black is threatening checkmate on b2 but White can take the *initiative* by sacrificing the Rook, as shown below. This sacrifice is simple and effective, and it involves no risk. Black's moves are forced, so White is sure of immediate compensation for the Rook. Remember though, even a simple sacrifice needs careful planning.

White plays **1. Rh8+!** This forces Black to take the Rook with **1...Kxh8** and diverts the action away from the vulnerable White King.

The White Queen then puts the Black King in check (**2. Qh5+**), and Black is forced to play **2...Kg8**. White now traps the King with **3. Qh7++**.

DID YOU KNOW?

- The word 'checkmate' derives from the Persian 'shah mat', meaning 'the King is dead'.

- In 1985, the Soviet player Gary Kasparov became the youngest World Champion ever at the age of 22 years, 210 days.

Intuitive sacrifice

The next few pages show a game played in 1984 by David Norwood, the author of this book and Saeed Saeed, an *International Grandmaster*. The game features an intuitive sacrifice which, together with a subsequent calculative sacrifice, wins the game for David Norwood. Norwood is playing Black and Saeed is playing White.

The game opens with a version of the Modern Benoni opening.* Both sides lose a Pawn in the struggle for central control and they both castle and *fianchetto*.

Black's plan is to exploit his Queenside strength and White wants to control the centre by bringing a Knight to c4. White's tenth move prepares for this by preventing Black from moving a Pawn to b5.

1. d4, Nf6; 2. c4, e6; 3. Nc3, c5; 4. d5, exd5.

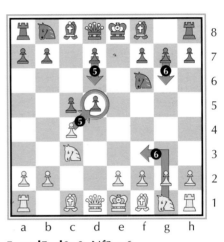

5. cxd5, d6; 6. Nf3, g6.

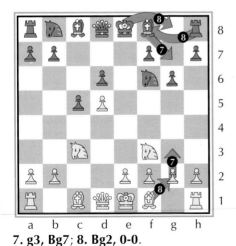

7. g3, Bg7; 8. Bg2, 0-0.

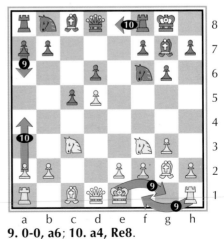

9. 0-0, a6; 10. a4, Re8.

A slightly different version of this opening appears on page 36.

The game continues

11. Nd2, Nbd7; 12. h3, Rb8; 13. Nc4, Ne5; 14. Na3...

In moves 11 and 13, White manoeuvres his Knight to square c4. From here it puts pressure on square d6, covers square e5 in readiness for a central Pawn advance and keeps guard on the Queenside.

By playing **13. Ne5**, Black forces White's Knight to leave its good position on c4. If White replied to this by moving **14. Nxe5**, Black would recapture with the Rook.

The White Knight has little function on the a3 square, other than to discourage Black from moving a Pawn to b5. However, White is planning to put Pawns on f4 and then e4, so that

the Black Knight will retreat. After this, the White Knight will be able to resume its powerful position on c4.

Black's intuitive sacrifice

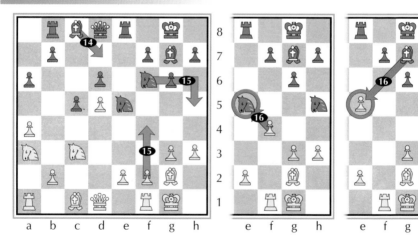

14...Bd7; 15. f4, Nh5.

16. fxe5.

16...Bxe5.

Black cannot prevent White's planned Pawn advance to f4, so he reacts tactically with an intuitive sacrifice. By playing **14...Bd7**, Black removes the one retreat square available to the e5 Knight so that, after White plays **15. f4**, the Knight will be lost. Next, Black moves the f6 Knight to h5 so that White can capture it with **16. fxe5**. Now, the Black Bishop can take the Pawn on e5. This leaves Black a Knight for a Pawn down.

Why Black sacrificed the Knight

Black's Knight sacrifice yields no immediate benefit. However, it has left Black in a very strong position, as can be seen by studying the state of play on the board below.

Analysing the position of each side regarding piece mobility, Pawn structure, King position and possible future plans will help to clarify Black's motives for sacrificing the Knight.

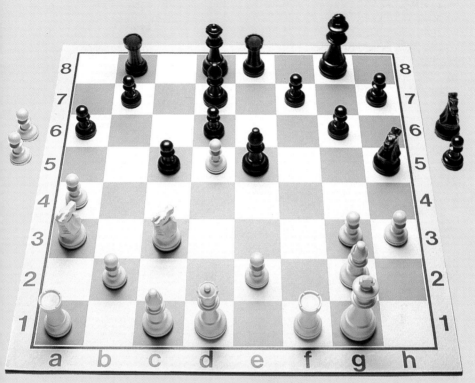

Black has:

- Captured two Pawns.
- Very good mobile pieces which control *open files* and diagonals.
- Several good plans – he can advance on the Queenside by putting a Pawn on b5, or he can play for a Kingside attack.
- Pressure on the important g3 Pawn. This Pawn covers the King and cannot be defended. If it moves to g4, the Black Knight can move to g3 and attack the White Rook.

White has:

- Captured a Pawn and a Knight.
- Weak pieces on the board, none of which are placed in useful attacking positions.
- No real plan. White's main plan to move the Pawn back to e5 is no longer feasible since it relied on the support of the f-Pawn, which is now lost.
- Bad Pawn structure with three *Pawn islands*.
- A semi-vulnerable King.

The game concludes

17. g4, Ng3.

White moves the g-Pawn to prevent Black from playing **17...Nxg3**, as this would leave Black only a point down on *material* and expose the White King. Such gains would be good compensation for the Knight sacrifice.

White's Rook on f1 is open to attack. However, if White moved it with **18. Rf2**, for example, then after **18...b5**, Black would have a good return for his sacrifice, threatening to move a Pawn to b4 to fork the Knights and advance the f-Pawn to open up the Kingside. The Black Queen could also join the attack by moving to h4.

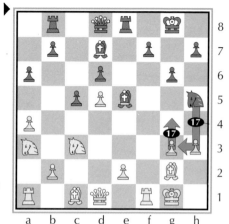

18. Nc4, Bxc3.

Instead of moving the f1 Rook, White moves the a3 Knight to guard against Black's Queenside threats. This forces Black to change plans and capture the Knight rather than the Rook. If Black had taken the Rook, **18...Nxf1** would have led to **19. Nxe5, Rxe5; 20.Qxf1**. Material would then be equal but Black would have lost his two best attacking pieces – the Knight and the black-squared Bishop.

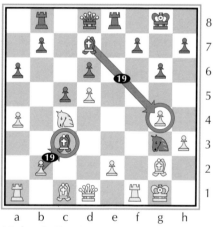

19. bxc3, Bxg4.

White recaptures with the Pawn. Black then takes the g4 Pawn and, in doing so, offers his Bishop as another powerful sacrifice. This is not an intuitive, but a calculative sacrifice as it is intended to yield immediate benefit.

Can you see what the consequences will be if White accepts the sacrifice of the Black Bishop? The answer is on the opposite page.

White takes the Bishop

20. hxg4, Nxe2+.

If White takes the Bishop, Black takes the Pawn and puts the King in check. Now, wherever the King moves it cannot escape ultimate checkmate as the Black Queen and Knight can work together to form a *mating net*. For example:

- If White plays **21. Kf2**, as below, then Black will achieve checkmate with **21...Qh4+; 22. Kf3, Qg3++.**

- If White plays **21. Kh2**, as below centre, this will lead to **21...Qh4+; 22. Bh3, Qg3+; and 23. Kh1, Qxh3++,** as shown bottom right.

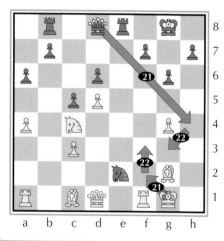

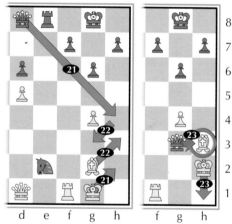

White leaves the Bishop

In fact Saeed did not accept the sacrifice of the Bishop. Even so, he could not save himself. The game continued with: **20. Qd3, Nxe2+; 21. Kh2, Nxc1; 22. Rfxc1, Be2!** White then resigned because, as soon as the Queen moved, Black could take the Knight. This would leave Black three Pawns up. In a Master-level game, this is usually enough to win.

> **DID YOU KNOW?**
>
> - In the Middle Ages, chess was considered too easy, so more complex versions were invented. One, Tamarlane's Chess, used a board with 110 squares. The pieces included camels and giraffes.
>
> - The longest recorded chess match, between Yedael Stepak and Yaacov Mashian in 1981, lasted 193 moves.

51

Where to go from here

The most effective way to improve your game is to practise. Family and friends may be good opponents to begin with but as your standard improves it is advisable to stretch yourself by playing a wider range of players. These two pages suggest ways to find challenging opponents and learn from your experience.

Chess clubs

The best place to find other chess players is a local chess club. Chess is popular worldwide, so there should be a club near where you live. Libraries can usually provide contact addresses, or you could write to your national chess federation, listed on the right.

Correspondence chess

Another way to increase the variety of your opponents is by playing correspondence chess. This involves writing down your move and posting it to your opponent, who posts back their reply. Again, contact your chess federation for details of other players.

Chess computers

There is a huge range of chess computers on the market, for players of all levels. Many have different settings so you can increase the degree of difficulty as your standard improves. Most computers are in the form of mini-boards with magnetic sensors to register the moves. Chess programs are also available for personal computers.

Chess computers are becoming ever more sophisticated. Each year the World Microcomputer Championship is held as a challenge between the top programs. The most powerful to date is called Deep Thought. It has defeated several Grandmasters but has so far been unable to beat the current World Champion, Gary Kasparov.

Contact addresses

British Chess Federation
9a Grand Parade
St Leonards-on-Sea
East Sussex
TN38 ODD
Great Britain

English Chess Association
London Chess Centre
58 St John's Hill
London
SW11 1SF
Great Britain

The Chess Federation of Canada
2212 Gladwin Crescent E-1
Ottawa
Ontario
K1B SN1
Canada

Australian Chess Federation
c/o Larry Ermacora
GPO Box 148
Sydney
NSW 2001
Australia

New Zealand Chess Association
PO Box 40-484
Upper Hutt
Wellington
New Zealand

United States Chess Federation
Attn. Al Lawrence
186 Route 9 West
New Windsor
NY 12550
USA

Books, magazines and videos

Reading chess literature is a very effective way of increasing your knowledge of theory. There are thousands of books available, covering every aspect of chess, so the choice can be confusing. Avoid anything too specialized to begin with but look instead for general books; one on the openings and one on endgames would be a suitable start. It is also a good idea to have an up-to-date book of chess rules, as there are more than you think and they do change from time to time.

National newspaper columns are a good source of information if you want to keep abreast of international chess events. Some publish regular chess puzzles.

Specialist chess magazines are another excellent source of information. They usually list the addresses of useful contacts and suppliers.

Chess videos are available too, for those who want to see the experts in action.

Chess publishers

These publishers distribute chess literature worldwide. You can write to them for catalogues and details of your nearest stockist.

▶

Pergamon Chess
Railway Road
Sutton Coldfield
B73 6AZ
England

B T Batsford Ltd
4 Fitzhardinge Street
London
W1H 0AH
England

Learning from mistakes

As you increase your range of opponents, it is important to keep a record of the games you have played. The best way to do this is to write down all your moves, and those of your opponent, as they are made, using *algebraic notation* (see page 5). It is possible to buy score sheets like those shown here, but any piece of paper will do. Recording your games in this way will help you to identify recurring themes and recognize repeated mistakes.

It is also a good idea, as soon as you have finished a game, to analyse it with your opponent. Discuss one another's opening strategies and plans. A post-mortem is especially useful if you have lost. Ask your opponent where you went wrong – you may learn how to win next time.

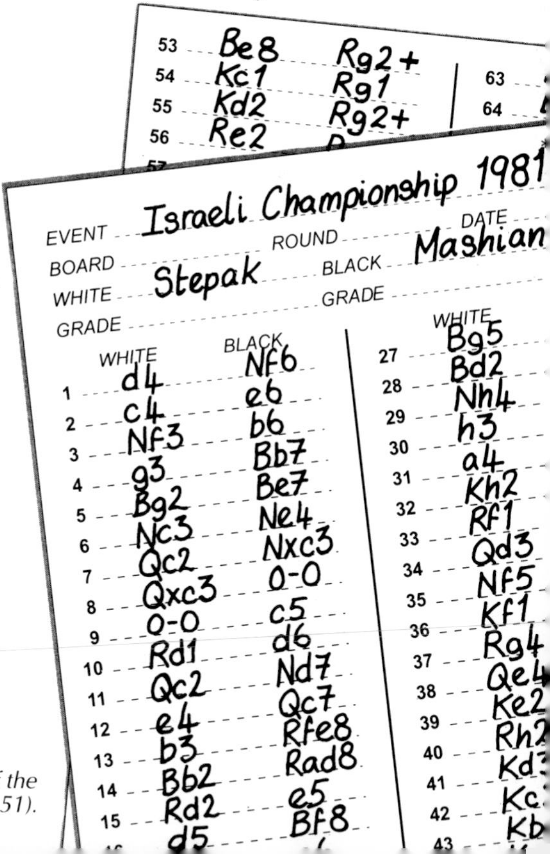

* This score sheet shows part of the longest recorded game (see page 51).

53	Be8	Rg2+	63
54	Kc1	Rg1	64
55	Kd2	Rg2+	
56	Re2		

Israeli Championship 1981

EVENT ___ Israeli Championship 1981
ROUND ___ DATE
BOARD ___ BLACK ___ Mashian
WHITE ___ Stepak ___ GRADE
GRADE

	WHITE	BLACK		WHITE
				Bg5
1	d4	Nf6	27	Bd2
2	c4	e6	28	Nh4
3	Nf3	b6	29	h3
4	g3	Bb7	30	a4
5	Bg2	Be7	31	Kh2
6	Nc3	Ne4	32	Rf1
7	Qc2	Nxc3	33	Qd3
8	Qxc3	0-0	34	Nf5
9	0-0	c5	35	Kf1
10	Rd1	d6	36	Rg4
11	Qc2	Nd7	37	Qe4
12	e4	Qc7	38	Ke2
13	b3	Rfe8	39	Rh2
14	Bb2	Rad8	40	Kd1
15	Rd2	e5	41	Kc1
	d5	Bf8	42	Kb1
			43	

Competitive chess

Once you have joined a chess club you will find out about the chess events and competitions in which you can take part. These two pages explain some of the procedures involved in chess tournaments. Opposite is a brief guide to gradings, and international chess.

How a tournament is run

Chess tournaments usually take place at weekends in chess clubs or town halls. Entrants are graded according to ability and play against a range of maybe five or six opponents. One point is awarded for a win and half for a draw. Winners play winners with similar scores and losers play losers. The entrant who gains the most points is the overall winner.

Time controls and chess clocks

In most competitions you will be required to play to a time limit. Each player has a specific amount of time in which to play a certain number of moves. To keep accurate track of your time you will need to use a chess clock, like the one shown here. This is a stop-clock with two faces, one to record the time you spend on your moves and one for your opponent's time. Both players set their clocks to the specified time limit. If it is your move, your clock will be ticking but your opponent's will be still. As soon as you have moved, press your clock button to stop your clock and set your

Flag drops when time is up.

opponent's ticking. If you run out of time before completing the required number of moves, you automatically lose the game.

It is up to you to notice if your opponent runs out of time, so watch out for this and keep quiet if your own time is up.

Time control tips

• When you play under a time control remember that you are fighting the clock as well as your opponent.

• Don't try to be a perfectionist, but play as good a move as possible in the time available.

• Don't spend too much time thinking about simple moves.

• Play at a steady pace; do not play too quickly but avoid being left with so little time that you have to rush your later moves. This may lead to silly mistakes.

• Be confident of your opening strategy. If you play through this quickly you will save time for later in the game.

Ending the game

There are several ways to win or draw in a game of chess. Checkmate is the ideal ending but very few advanced games actually come to this. Below are some of the more common ways for a game to end.

Offering a draw

At *Master* level the most common conclusion to a game is for one of the players to offer a draw. A draw can be offered at any point during the game but should really be suggested only if the positions are equal and neither side can gain the advantage. Beware of offering a draw if you stand any chance at all of winning.

Resigning

One sure way to lose a game is to resign. Some players do this when they feel that their position is so hopeless that it is pointless to continue. A player may indicate their resignation by tipping over their own King. It is never a good idea to resign, however, as even the most experienced player can make a blunder and even if you cannot win you may be able to play for *stalemate*.

Ways to win and draw

Win	checkmate
	opponent resigns
	opponent runs out of time
Draw	stalemate
	agreed draw
	perpetual check
	both players run out of time*
	three-fold repetition of position**

National ratings

When a tournament is organized, it is usually registered with the national chess federation. Once a player begins to compete regularly in these registered tournaments, he or she is given a rating according to performance against other rated players. Each country has its own national rating system, organized by its chess federation. The systems vary a great deal – a player may begin with a rating of 60 in one country and 200 in another. Ratings lists are usually published annually or biannually so you can measure your progress by seeing how much your rating has gone up (or down).

International chess

Above the various national rating structures is a standardized international rating system, which a player enters if he or she begins to compete at international level. This rating system is organized by *FIDE* (Fédération Internationale des Echecs), the governing body for worldwide chess. FIDE also awards the titles *FIDE Master*, *International Master*, or higher than this, *International Grandmaster*, to those people who have played consistently well against other world-class players.

Professional chess

Top chess players are paid to take part in the important tournaments and substantial prize money is awarded. This means that some players can make chess their career. Most professional players write books and articles to supplement their income but a few are able to exist solely by playing the game.

* This can only occur if one player fails to realize that the other has run out of time.
** This is when the players reach the same position three times in a row.

Glossary

The list of words on the next few pages explains chess terms used in this book. The page numbers in brackets direct you to the place in the book where the glossary word is most clearly defined.

Algebraic notation A method of recording chess moves using letters for the pieces and grid references for their positions. (Page 5)

Back rank mate Checkmate by a Queen or Rook along the eighth rank, where the King is blocked in by its own Pawns. (Page 40)

Backward Pawn A Pawn that has trailed behind and is no longer supported by other Pawns. (Page 13)

Bad-squared Bishop A Bishop that is blocked by its own Pawns because the Pawns are positioned on squares of the same colour as the Bishop's square. (Page 6)

Calculative sacrifice Allowing a piece to be captured in order to gain immediate benefit in terms of **material**, mobility or attacking potential. (Page 46)

Castling A manoeuvre in which the King moves two squares towards the side of the board and the Rook jumps over the King. Neither piece must have moved from its starting position and there must be no pieces between them. Castling cannot take place if the King has to pass over a square that is attacked by the enemy. (Page 5)

Closed file A **file** blocked by both Black and White Pawns. (Page 39)

Combination A planned series of moves which is intended to force certain responses from the opponent, and lead them into an undesirable position. (Page 42)

Connected Pawns Pawns adjacent to one another.

Counter gambit A strategy in which a minor piece or Pawn is offered for **sacrifice** in response to an earlier gambit (piece offered for sacrifice) by the opponent. (Page 19)

Discovered attack A tactic where one piece is moved to reveal an attack by another piece.

Discovered check A tactic where one piece moves so that a piece behind it can give check. (Page 42)

Double check   When a piece moves to put the enemy King in check, revealing a second check by a piece behind it. (Page 63)

Double Pawns   Two Pawns of the same colour positioned one in front of the other. (Page 13)

Double Rooks   Two Rooks of the same colour positioned on the same **rank** or **file**. (Page 7)

Endgame   The closing stage of a game, when few pieces are left on the board. (Page 4)

Equalize   Make a move that balances the strengths and weaknesses of either side, so that, at that point, both sides have an equal chance of winning. (Page 21)

Exchange   Trading a piece for an enemy piece, or pieces, of equal value. (Page 9)

Exchange advantage   Trading a piece for an enemy piece, or pieces, of greater value. (Page 9)

Fair exchange   Same as **Exchange**. Trading a piece for an enemy piece, or pieces, of equal value.

Fianchetto   A manoeuvre that develops the Bishop to a position from which it controls the longest diagonal. (Page 6)

FIDE   Fédération Internationale des Echecs. The world chess federation which organizes the international rating system, awards and titles. (Page 55)

FIDE Master   Title awarded by FIDE, ranked below **International Master**. (Page 55)

File   A column of squares running from the top of the board to the bottom. The files are lettered a–h in notation. (Page 5)

Fixed Pawn   A Pawn whose advance is blocked by an enemy piece. (Page 13)

Forced mate   A sequence of moves that will lead to checkmate, irrespective of the opponent's responses.

Fork   A simultaneous attack on two pieces by one enemy piece. (Page 43)

Gambit	An opening strategy, offering the sacrifice of a **minor piece**, or Pawn, in order to achieve good development. (Page 18)
Good-squared Bishop	A Bishop that is mobile because it is positioned on a square of the opposite colour to the squares on which most of its Pawns are stationed. (Page 6)
Hanging Pawns	Two Pawns on adjacent **files** that have no enemy Pawns ahead of them and no friendly Pawns on the files to either side. (Page 13)
Initiative, have the	To lead the game with threatening moves so that your opponent has to respond defensively. (Page 15)
International Grandmaster	A title awarded by FIDE for consistent excellent play at international level. (Page 55)
International Master	A title awarded by FIDE. Not as high a title as **International Grandmaster**. (Page 55)
Intuitive sacrifice	Surrendering a piece in order to gain the advantage in the long term, but bringing no immediate benefit. (Page 47)
Isolated Pawn	A Pawn that has no neighbouring Pawns on the **files** adjacent to it. (Page 13)
Kingside	**Files** e–h on the board. (Page 4)
Lose a tempo	Neglect to make a move within an active area of the board; this may sometimes be intentional as it can strengthen your position. (Page 29)
Major piece	A Queen or Rook. (Page 13)
Material	The total value in points of a player's pieces on the board. (Page 9)
Material advantage	Greater strength in terms of the value of the pieces on the board. (Page 10)
Material disadvantage	Less strength than your opponent in terms of the total value of your pieces on the board. (Page 9)
Mating net	Pieces working together to trap and checkmate the enemy King. (Page 32)

Middlegame	The stage of the game after the opening and before the **endgame**, when most pieces are **exchanged**. (Page 4)
Minor piece	A Bishop or Knight.
Open file	A **file** on which there are no Pawns. A file is still open even if it is occupied by pieces other than Pawns. (Page 7)
Opening	The first stage of a game, from move one until piece development is complete. (Page 4)
Opposition, have the	To move your King so that it faces the enemy King on the same **file** with only one square separating them, so the enemy King has to move back or sideways. (Page 29)
Overloaded	A piece which is defending too many pieces at once. (Page 24)
Passed Pawn	A Pawn that will not encounter enemy Pawns on its own or an adjacent **file** on its way to the other end of the board. (Page 12)
Pawn break	The possibility of opening up a blocked **Pawn structure** by advancing a Pawn.
Pawn centre	A pair or group of Pawns of the same colour that occupy the central squares of the board. (Page 23)
Pawn chain	A string of two or more Pawns of the same colour along a diagonal. (Page 12)
Pawn island	A Pawn or group of Pawns separated from other Pawns of the same colour. (Page 12)
Pawn structure	The arrangement of a player's Pawns on the board. (Page 11)
Perpetual check	When a player is put in check repeatedly but cannot be checkmated. In this event the game is agreed drawn.
Piece	Any chess piece other than the Pawn, but usually referring to a Knight or Bishop.
Pin	An attack on a piece that is shielding another piece of greater value. The pinned piece must remain in position or else expose the more valuable piece to attack. (Page 43)

Positional advantage	Pieces positioned so that they have more mobility and potential than those of the opponent. Key factors are good **Pawn structure**, control of **open files** and diagonals, and a mobile Bishop. (Page 17)
Promote a Pawn	Make a Pawn into a more powerful piece (usually a Queen, or sometimes a Knight) when it reaches the other end of the board. (Page 28)
Queening square	The square which a Pawn must reach in order for it to **promote**. (Page 29)
Queenside	**Files** a–d on the board. (Page 5)
Rank	A row of squares running across the board, numbered 1–8 in notation. (Page 5)
Resign	To admit defeat when you think you cannot win. (Page 57)
Sacrifice	To lose a piece of greater value than the one you capture. (Page 9)
Semi-open file	A **file** in front of a Queen or Rook that is occupied by just one enemy Pawn and none of your own. A file is still semi-open even if it contains pieces other than the Pawn. (Page 37)
Skewer	An attack which forces a valuable piece to move and so reveals an attack on a piece of less value.
Smothered mate	Checkmate with a Knight when the King is blocked in by its own pieces. (Page 63)
Space advantage	Controlling a greater area of the board, allowing more space to manoeuvre.
Stalemate	A situation where the player whose turn it is next can make no legal move but is not in check. This ends the game immediately as a draw. (Page 33)
Trade	*See* **Exchange**.
Triple Pawns	Three Pawns of the same colour positioned along a **file**, one in front of the other. (Page 13)
Underpromote	**Promote a Pawn** to a piece other than a Queen. (Page 62)

Puzzle answers

Page 10

1. White is stronger. The White Knight is mobile but the Black Bishop is blocked in by its own Pawns.

2. Black should move **1...Nxd3**. The Knight will then be taken by the White Queen but Black will have the *exchange advantage* and the stronger position. White will be left with a *bad-squared Bishop* which is unable to attack Black's strong, centrally placed Knight.

3. Black should move the Queen to a5, putting the White King in check. Black then has to move out of check and the White Queen can take the Bishop on g5.

4. White should move the Queen to d4 to put the Black King in check. Black is then forced to move the King and the White Queen can capture the b2 Rook.

5. White should move **1. Bh3** to attack the ▶ Black Knight. The Knight will be forced to remain in position to shield the Rook on c8 – this is called a *pin*. If Black tries to defend with **1...Rd8**, then **2. Nc6** will ensure that the Knight is captured.

6. Black can play **1...Rh1**, moving the Rook to put the White King in check. White is forced to move the King to the g-file. Black can then force the King back to the h-file ▼

Page 27

1. Black should play **1...Rc2**. With this move the Rook attacks both the White Pawn and Queen. When the Queen moves out of danger the Rook can capture the Pawn.

2. White should capture the black-squared Bishop on g7. Most of the Black Pawns are on white squares, so this Bishop is very powerful.

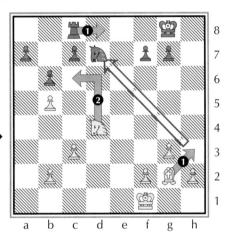

with **2...Rg1** and go on to capture the Knight with **3...Rxg8**.

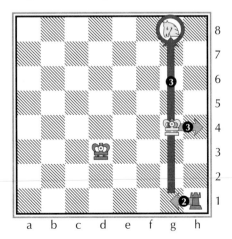

Puzzle answers continued

Page 31

If White moved the Rook from the a-file, the Black Rook could leave its defending position and the a2 Pawn could *promote*.

If the White King moved **1. Kf3**, this would allow Black's Pawn to promote with **1...Rf1+; 2. Ke3, a1(Q)**.

▼

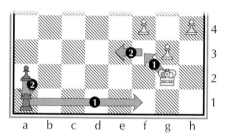

If, on the other hand, White moved **1. Kf2**, the White Rook would be lost with **1...Rh1!; 2. Rxa2, Rh2+; 3. Kg1, Rxa2.**

▼

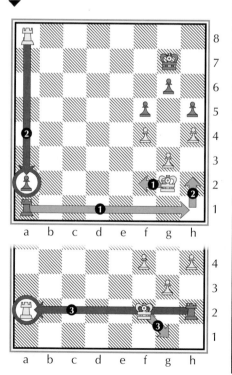

Page 34

1. White should play **1. h3** as this leads to **1...Kh8; 2. h4, Kg8; 3. h5, Kh8; 4. g6, hxg6; 5. hxg6, Kg8; 6. g7, Kf7** and the Pawn can now promote, as shown below. (Note that if White played **1. h4**, this would lead to **1...Kh8; 2. h5, Kg8; 3. g6, hxg6; 4. hxg6, Kh8=**.)

▼

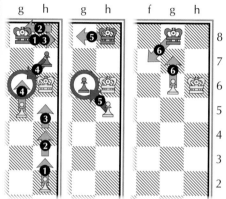

2. White should *underpromote* with **1. e8(N)+**. If White promoted to a Queen, Black would give checkmate with **1...Ra8**. By promoting to a Knight, White puts the Black King in check and forces it to move. This breaks the *mating net*, which relied on the two Kings facing each other. Now, with accurate play, White can draw.

▼

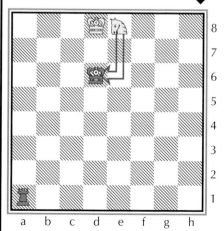

Page 37

Black can support the b-Pawn by putting a Rook on b8. White can support the Pawn advance to e5 by moving the d2 Knight to c4 or f3 and bringing the Rook to e1.

▼

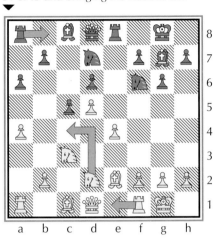

Page 39

1. White could bring both Rooks to the d-file, put a Bishop on f3 and attack the pieces which are defending Black's d5 Pawn.

2.The King is exposed along the g-file so it would be a good idea to put a Rook on this file. The best way to do this would be to play **1. Re3** followed by **2. Rg3+**.

▼

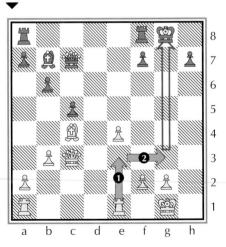

Page 45

1. White should play **1. Rxe7**. This tactic involves *overloading* the f8 Bishop – it cannot defend the Knight on e7 and guard against checkmate from g7 too. After **1...Bxe7**, White can play **2. Qg7++**.

▼

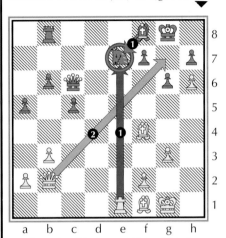

2. White should play **1. Nh6+**. This is a *double check* – the Knight has put the King in check and revealed a *discovered check* by the Queen. The King must move **1...Kh8**. Now White can play **2. Qg8+** and the Rook is forced to capture the Queen (**2...Rxg8**). Now White can move **3. Nf7++**. This is called a *smothered mate* as the checkmated King is hemmed-in by its own pieces.

▼

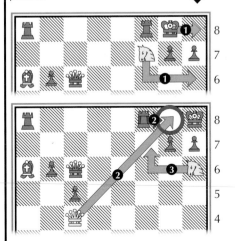

Index

Page numbers printed in italics indicate glossary references.